CASTLES
IN THE AIR
and Other Tales

Books by Stephen Krensky

For the students at Wellington,

Happy reading!

Stephen Krensky

Stephen Krensky

CASTLES
IN THE AIR
and Other Tales

Drawings by Warren Lieberman

Atheneum   1979   New York

For Lynne and Diane

LIBRARY OF CONGRESS CATALOGING IN PUBLICATION DATA

Krensky, Stephen.   Castles in the air.

SUMMARY: Five clichés woven into stories. Included are
"Too Clever for Words," "Barrel of Fun,"
"Fine Kettle of Fish," and "The Last Straw."
[1. Humorous stories]   I. Lieberman, Warren.
II. Title.
PZ7.K883Cas   [Fic]   78-11836
ISBN 0-689-30684-9

Copyright © 1979 by Stephen Krensky
All rights reserved
Published simultaneously in Canada by
McClelland & Stewart, Ltd.
Manufactured by The American Book–Stratford Press
Saddle Brook, New Jersey
Designed by Mary M. Ahern
First Edition

Contents

CASTLES
IN THE AIR
and Other Tales

Castles in the Air

A LONG TIME AGO, there lived a king newly come to the throne. He was not a young man, however, for his father had ruled for many years. As was the custom, he settled major disputes within the kingdom, hunted wild boars in the forest, and hosted sumptuous banquets on important holidays. His chief delight, though, was not his official duties, but his inventions. The king tinkered endlessly with every kind of mechanical device and building structure, sometimes successfully and sometimes not. His castle and the countryside were littered with abandoned projects.

As was also the custom, the king wooed princesses both near and far, each one more beautiful than the last. He was ill at ease making flowery speeches or giving costly gifts; the only things he readily exchanged were his ideas. The princesses, though, rather liked receiving flowery compliments and priceless baubles, and a daydreaming king was no substitute for that.

BEYOND THE VILLAGE surrounding the royal castle, a spinster had settled in a small cottage. She was not rich or pretty, but decidedly clever, being especially skilled in magical lore. Hopeful heroes flocked daily to her door for help. They were handsome fellows, resplendent in their armor, who had sworn to fight a dragon, giant, or the like for the love of a fair maiden. The battles to come were all they spoke of. Though the spinster aided them in her fashion, she never envied the fair maidens.

If heroes were nothing more than ruddy cheeks and strong sword arms, then she could do without them.

Most often her visitors came and went on the post road nearby. It was heavily traveled, but sadly neglected, and now stood pockmarked with holes. Stumbling horses threw down a great many riders, all of whom beseeched her for assistance. This troubled the spinster. Healing balms were expensive, and she could ill afford to spare the time from her work.

Yet not until a disabled carriage put into her care six flustered passengers at once did she finally lose her temper. And lost it remained. Since only the king had the resources to improve the road to her liking, to the king she would go.

THE ROYAL CASTLE was larger up close than she had imagined it from afar. Taking a deep breath, she strode across the drawbridge into a bustling courtyard.

"Bring me to the king!" she snapped to a liveried page.

He was trained to follow orders and led her immediately to the throne room. The polished tables, thick tapestries and golden candelabras furnished an imposing setting, but the spinster hardly noticed. Her attention was drawn to the king, who was sitting on the floor next to a pile of blocks.

"Good afternoon, Your Majesty," she said, remembering her manners.

"Ssssssh," he replied, forgetting his entirely. Without glancing up, he went on stacking blocks on top of each other. They shortly began to sway and, despite the king's protests, soon toppled over. He muttered to himself and called for more blocks.

The spinster was tapped on the shoulder.

"I'm afraid the king is not giving audiences today," said his trusted chief advisor. "He has been studying towers of late and is consumed by the notion of building one with three turrets."

Towers and turrets were not her concern, but the spinster was intrigued by the king's fervor. She left quietly, promising to come back on the morrow.

True to her word, the spinster returned the next day. This time there were no blocks in the throne room. Instead, the king was sitting amid a mound of papers that were covered with sketches and notes. A quill sat limply in his hand.

The spinster curtsied. "Your Majesty," she said. "I ask a boon. The road near my cottage is marred by ruts and holes. It grows more dangerous with every rainfall. Could you please see to its repair?"

The king began to scribble while she spoke

and continued to write after she had stopped. His nose was wrinkled and the creases ran deep in his forehead. It was not a heroic face, the spinster decided, but she warmed to it, nonetheless.

"Why are you blushing?" the king demanded, abruptly crushing a flawed design.

The spinster stammered something about the heat.

"Oh," he said. "Now, what was it you wanted? Ah, yes, I remember. A dangerous road. Repairs and so forth." He reflected briefly. "Not much flair in that."

"Flair has its place, Sire, but I do need your help."

Her reproachful tone surprised the king. He was about to respond when a sudden thought sent him burrowing through the papers. "That could do it!" he cried. "Might be the proper balance . . . compensates for the wind. Bring back the blocks, I say!"

The forgotten spinster was again escorted out by the chief advisor. "You understand, of course," he said, "that His Majesty is a dedicated inventor." He smiled graciously. "And after all, it is his right to build castles in the air."

The spinster stared ahead angrily. "If that's what he wants," she murmured, "it can be arranged."

SEVERAL DAYS LATER, the king returned from a hunt to find his chief advisor anxiously awaiting him.

"Sire," he said, "I bear strange tidings. The duke's castle is floating hundreds of feet above the ground."

The king was impressed, though not a little puzzled. "How did the duke contrive such a feat?" he wondered, shaking his head. "I can't even manage that tower. Perhaps the duke doesn't use blocks."

"It was not his idea, Sire. The duke has

dropped repeated messages to that effect from the walls. In fact, he seems to think it's something you arranged." The chief advisor paused. "As you recall, the duke is rather excitable."

The king sighed. "I only wish I was responsible. Still, I must see the castle for myself. Ready a fresh horse at once."

The king was gone all afternoon. When he did return, his face glowed with excitement. He wandered through the halls telling everyone what a remarkable sight he had witnessed. One of the pages found him in the kitchen describing the scene in great detail to the cooks and scullery maids.

The page announced a visitor.

"Very well," said the king. "I'll be up in a moment."

It was the spinster who awaited him. Her manner was assured, her eyes sparkling with confidence. The king knew princesses whose eyes glittered on occasion, but sparkling was another thing entirely.

"This is a great day," he announced. "Truly historic. We have a castle in the air, you know."

"I know," said the spinster. "I put it there."

The king clapped his hands. "You accomplished this marvel?" he cried. "What imagination!" He beckoned her forward. "Come tell me how it's done."

The spinster was confused. The heroes she knew would feel threatened by a floating castle, not pleased by it. "I am not here to share secrets," she declared. "I simply want the post road repaired."

The king waved his hand impatiently. "Never mind that," he ordered. "We have no time for roads. Now, about the castle. How did you ever manage it?"

The spinster folded her arms and said nothing.

The king was astounded. "Take this woman to the dungeon," he fumed, his royal pride surfacing vengefully. "A night there will change her mind."

THAT EVENING, a troupe of jugglers performed for the king. He usually watched their tricks in earnest, always sure a ball would fall or a plate would drop, though none ever did. The present entertainment, however, could not ease the strange discontent he felt. And the balls sparkling in the candlelight served only to remind him of sparkling eyes in the dungeon below.

The king retired early to his bedchamber. There the silence lay heavily about, unbroken save by his occasional mutterings. The king's thoughts churned from one to another like cream into butter, but none of them were any comfort to him. Weariness overcame him at last, and he slept fitfully till dawn.

Sunrise found the chief advisor rushing into the royal bedchamber without knocking. The king opened his eyes, noted the distraught face of his trusted minister, and burrowed under a quilt.

"The most dreadful thing has happened, Sire. I don't know what to do. We're . . . we're floating."

The king uncovered his head. He tumbled to the floor as the castle swayed in the wind, sending his fourposter bed sliding back and forth. His dresser drawers fell out, spilling shirts and breeches onto the rug. Fortunately, the king was an accomplished sailor. Steadying his feet on the deck of his bedchamber, he walked to the window.

Far beneath him lay the castle moat, the village stretching out around it. Farmhouses sat like intricate toys on patchwork squares, tied together by brown ribbon roads. The sea and the mountains met in the distance, the beginning of one and the ending of the other indistinguishable in the haze.

The king nodded to himself and sighed.

"Are you all right, Your Majesty?" the chief advisor asked.

The king turned almost reluctantly from the window. He smiled nervously. "Bring the prisoner to the throne room," he ordered. "And see that we're not disturbed."

The spinster had been anticipating the royal summons, and she entered the throne room prepared for a burst of the king's temper. She was determined to have her own way, but she was a little sorry the three-turreted tower couldn't be part of the conversation. She had several suggestions to make.

Instead of the angry shout she expected, however, the king simply stared at her. There was nothing absent-minded about his expression; indeed, rarely had he looked so composed.

The spinster found his glance unsettling.

"Have you reconsidered my request?" she asked.

The king was silent.

"I should add that until you see reason the castle will not descend. You will be able to give the matter your full attention."

"That could be inconvenient," said the king, approaching her. "But bearable, I think, if you would be by my side." He gently took her hand.

Whatever the spinster's initial reaction, the king proved quite persuasive in the end. Their marriage took place a fortnight after the two castles returned to the ground. In future years, the roads throughout the kingdom were inspected and repaired, while much else that needed mending was attended to as well. And on the site of the queen's former cottage, a splendid three-turreted tower was built, to the lasting admiration of everyone who passed it.

A Fine Kettle of Fish

A YOUNG FISHERMAN once lived in a gray-shingled cottage by the sea. In fair weather and foul, he sailed his boat out on the morning tide, casting his nets while the light held, and returning to the harbor at sunset. The fisherman knew the ocean's shallows and depths as well as he knew the contours of his own face, though he caught only enough fish to supply his simple needs.

One afternoon, when he was sailing his boat in, the fisherman was beset by a thick fog. It rolled across his prow, hiding both sun and shore in

17

swirling mists. Not till dusk did it lift. The fisherman reached the harbor late that day. Only a few merchants still remained, so he did not sell his entire catch.

The fisherman went home finally with a handful of copper coins and several fine fish,

which he decided to cook for his supper. After warming himself by the fire, he placed the fish in a gleaming kettle.

A knock at the door surprised him. Who could be calling at this hour?

"Hullo?" he shouted.

"Alms for the poor," said a meek voice.

The kindly fisherman opened the door.

But no beggar stood before him, only a ruthless thief who forced his way inside. He was terribly hungry, and having spied the fish from the window, he intended to steal them. The stout club he carried would brook no interference. Snatching the kettle, the thief glanced quickly around. The humble cottage held no other valuables.

"Tell nobody I was here," he snarled.

The tired fisherman nodded weakly. What was one supper compared to a stout club?

The thief bolted from sight as silently as he had come. He traveled far under the waxing moon, skillfully hiding his trail in passing. Owls hooted around him; bats fluttered by. Finally deeming it safe, he stopped to make a fire. "I will eat well tonight!" he exclaimed, licking his lips in delight. Roguishly twirling his moustache, he heaped more branches on the blaze. The flames reached up to consume them.

"Good fellow," said someone from beyond the trees, "might you share your supper with a stranger?"

The thief froze.

A smartly dressed soldier led his horse into the clearing. His eyes never left the kettle. "I saw your fire from afar," he continued, "and I have not eaten since morning."

The thief took proper note of the soldier's long sword. "Sit down, sit down," he said pleasantly. "There is plenty of fish for us both."

The grateful soldier turned to unsaddle his horse. The thief recovered his club. That gold brocade, he thought, would look well at his shoulders, and the horse would bring a fine price. He crept forward a step, passing before the fire. His shadow, though, leaped out ahead of him.

The soldier whirled. "Deceitful brigand!" he cried, the thief's intent too plain to ignore. He drew his sword. "Your treachery will cost you dearly."

"Maybe not," said the thief, swinging his club.

The nimble soldier jumped back.

For a time they parried back and forth, evenly matched in anger and skill. But like the failing fire, the thief tired at last. Treacherous battles he had fought aplenty; yet cunning would not serve him here. As the embers smouldered, the soldier's still flashing blade edged him out of the clearing.

"Stand your ground, coward!" the soldier declared.

The thief dodged a clever thrust, but caught his foot on a root. He fell to the ground, his head hitting a rock. The club dropped from his hand.

"Knocked senseless," muttered the soldier. "And lucky for him, too." He sheathed his sword.

"But I'll take the kettle for my trouble." He carried it to his horse, mounted unsteadily, and departed.

At the first crossroads, he came upon a large stone manor. Light-headed and weary, he rode to the front door. "Open up!" he shouted. "Open up, I say!"

The noise roused the household. The master of the manor, a wealthy merchant, heard the soldier's tale from his bedroom window and went downstairs. A trusted servant followed him out.

The soldier sat dazedly on his horse.

"Poor fellow," said the merchant. "You took quite a beating. Here, let me hold the heavy kettle." He took it brusquely. "So, this was the thief's treasure, eh? Extraordinary fish, no doubt."

The soldier nodded. But before he could dismount, the merchant signaled to his servant, who flicked a whip at horse and rider. The startled animal reared and galloped away toward the gate. The soldier clung dearly to the saddle.

"And don't come back," the merchant called after him, "or I'll set the dogs on you." Chuckling quietly, he put the kettle safely in the kitchen and returned to bed.

He awoke at noon. Shouting orders, he bathed and dressed, taking care that his best china and silver was laid out. "But which recipe . . ." he murmured, sticking a carnation in his lapel. He started downstairs to confer with the cook.

The sound of a carriage distracted him. "Oh, bother!" grumbled the merchant. He was not in an entertaining mood.

His butler announced the visitor.

"My Lord Chamberlain," the merchant gasped, a smile forcing its way across his face. "What happy circumstance brings you here?"

His distinguished guest brushed the dust from his shoulders. "The king has sent me to collect your taxes. I trust I have not traveled in vain."

The merchant reassured him on that point. "I'll have the chests brought to your carriage," he said.

The Lord Chamberlain took a pinch of snuff and strolled into the dining room. He ran a finger along the lace tablecloth, studied his reflection in the china, and tapped the crystal goblet. The bell-like tone almost filled the awkward silence. "Beautiful settings," he observed. "A special occasion, perhaps?"

"Not at all, Your Excellency. I, ah, simply acquired a fine kettle of fish for dinner." The merchant paused. "Would you care to join me?"

The Lord Chamberlain took another pinch of snuff. Such lavish attention was noteworthy, but the king would not think well of any delays. "I have no time," he replied. "A pity. Of course, you could part with the fish for my sake."

The merchant paled. His guest was known to throw people into the royal dungeon when they ignored his requests.

Five chests of gold were soon loaded on top of the carriage. The Lord Chamberlain followed behind, the kettle of fish in tow. He ordered the coachman to hurry. The meal to come consumed his thoughts. Even the lurching carriage could not dispel his jubilant mood.

The royal palace sat high on a hill, in sight of the sea and the forest. That afternoon, the king was looking out his highest tower, his hands clasped behind his back. The Lord Chamberlain was late, and the king was unhappy about it. The merchant's gold was much needed by his treasury.

"At last," he sighed, as the handsome carriage appeared in the distance. When it neared the gates, he dispatched one of the guards to fetch his minister directly.

The Lord Chamberlain had hoped to eat first, but he dutifully tucked the kettle under one arm and reported to the tower.

"Well?" the king demanded at his entrance.

"You may rest easy, Your Majesty. The gold is here."

"Good," said the king. He skeptically eyed the kettle.

"This is just a trifle, Sire. Hardly worth your interest."

"I'll judge that for myself."

The Lord Chamberlain hastened to explain. "It's merely some fish from the merchant."

The king's appetite stirred. The merchant had a well-known fondness for excellent food. "Let me see them," he ordered.

The Lord Chamberlain dared not refuse, and the kettle exchanged hands. Its appearance did not impress the king, so scuffed and smudged was it now. But the fish were the important thing. He opened the lid.

"Phew!"

The king hurriedly tossed the kettle out the window. "Rotten through and through," he muttered.

The kettle sailed over the palace walls. The fish fell out and were scattered by the wind, flopping loudly as they hit the cobblestone streets. The alley cats, who were not so particular, enjoyed them thoroughly.

The Last Straw

IN A THATCHED COTTAGE that was nothing more and nothing less than one large room, three brothers lived together. Dram was the oldest, a tall, lean fellow whose thirst was never quenched for long. A year younger was Gram, who was short, fat, and constantly hungry. Youngest of all was Driblet, who was neither tall nor short, fat nor thin, but quick-witted from years of scrounging for his own food and drink.

While Dram took pride in drinking and Gram thought well of eating, they each took a dim view of the other's achievements. Naturally, these objections surfaced at meals, generally beginning at breakfast.

"Where is the bread?" Dram would ask, searching through the cupboard. "There was a whole loaf here. Did you finish it, Gram?"

"What if I did?" Gram would reply, taking out an empty pitcher. "You certainly took care of the milk."

At lunch they argued about cheese and cider and at supper about beef and ale, but what followed was always the same. Like two large puppets, Dram and Gram would raise their heads and start to shout. Only the sight of more food and drink, which Driblet saved for such times, distracted them from further bickering.

Whatever their differences, though, they worked well together in the fields. On a day that they were plowing near the road, a farmer approached, leading a cow to market.

Gram nudged Dram in the side. "Is that poor excuse for an animal for sale?" he asked.

The indignant farmer turned to him. "Young fellow, you're no judge of livestock. A better cow never lived. The pride of my herd."

"It's a long way to market," said Dram.

"A hot and dusty trip," Gram added. "A lot of bother for a poor creature that looks as if she'll drop in the next mile."

The farmer hesitated.

The two brothers had soon made up so many flaws that the farmer was glad to sell the cow for a fraction of its worth. Dram and Gram returned home in high spirits, eager to show Driblet their prize.

He was properly impressed.

Gram patted the cow's flanks. "The beef on her will last a month," he remarked.

Dram stared at him. "What do you mean,

beef? We bought this cow for her milk. Three pails a day, I expect."

Now it was Gram who stared.

"Supper's ready," Driblet said quickly.

That calmed them for the moment, but half way through the meal, Dram and Gram reached for the same jug of ale.

"Let go!" said Gram. "You've had too much already."

Dram snarled at him, wrenched the jug free, and swallowed its contents.

Gram jumped to his feet, knocking over his chair. "That did it!" he cried.

"Easy there," said Driblet. "Pick up your chair and sit down."

Gram slowly picked up the chair—and threw it across the table.

Dram had the good sense to duck.

The chair crashed through a window. Even

before the glass fell, Dram hurled his plate in return. Beef and gravy splattered over Gram's shirt. As Driblet dove for cover, the air filled with dishes, mugs, candlesticks, and any loose furniture close by. Bags of flour and sugar were ripped open and emptied, leaving the room looking as if a light snow had fallen. In the midst of it, Dram and Gram wrestled until weariness overcame them both.

Driblet surveyed their handiwork in dismay. Had a giant sat on the roof and poked holes in the walls, it would have looked much the same. "Everything's ruined," he moaned.

"Who cares?" said Gram, breathing heavily. "I'm moving out."

Dram snorted. "So am I," he muttered.

A FORTNIGHT LATER, the walls of three new cottages had risen, each separated by a strip of forest from the others. Dram, Gram and Driblet then sold the troublesome cow in town, where they bought tables, chairs, cupboards, beds, and straw for the thatched roofs. It took all the money they had. Returning home, Dram and Gram parceled out the furniture while Driblet divided up the straw into three equal piles.

There was one strand remaining.

"We should each get a piece," said Gram.

"Idiot!" said Dram. "A little piece is useless. Only a long strand can be woven with the rest."

Driblet carefully put it aside. "Maybe it won't matter," he said.

The first night the roofs were in place, a fierce storm raged over the farm. Shafts of lightning drew cracks across the sky; thunderous bursts rattled the trees. The bitter wind whipped the rain against the ground, leaving islands of water behind.

At dawn, the storm passed. Outside Driblet's

cottage, a chirping bird was cut off by the sound of Dram's voice.

"Wake up!" he shouted angrily.

Driblet bounded out of bed and opened the door. Dram stalked in. "I hardly slept last night," he fumed. "The rain dripped in through a slit in my roof. I emptied a pail every hour. This can't go on. I need the last straw. Where is it?"

"Hold a moment," said Gram from the doorway. He eyed them blearily. "The wind blew in through a slit in my roof. I nearly froze. Clearly, the last straw should be mine."

"Nonsense," said Dram. "You are not important enough to get it. I can drink a barrel of water at one meal. Can you match that?"

"Why bother?" sneered Gram. "It's hardly important. Now, I can eat a suckling pig in a single day. That's noteworthy."

Driblet stepped between them and yawned.

"Both wind and rain came through a slit in my roof," he said. "So my claim to the last straw is the strongest of all."

His remark was met by gales of laughter. Dram and Gram were agreed on one thing—Driblet's claim was not worth mentioning.

Their younger brother did not enjoy the joke. "I have the best right to it," he insisted. "If you two could get along, we wouldn't need a straw, anyway. And eating or drinking a lot is impressive, perhaps, but to think that my own brothers make hollow boasts . . ."

"Hollow boasts?" they cried. This insult could not be ignored. Dram and Gram consulted briefly.

"Driblet," Dram said finally, "you have gone too far. We demand an apology."

"I'm not sorry," said Driblet. "I can prove what I said."

"Oh," said Dram. "Very well, then. If you can

prove that I am not a great drinker . . ."

"And that I am not a great eater," said Gram.

"Then the last straw is yours," Dram finished. He smiled craftily. "Fail, though, and you must choose which of us will get it. The loser will give you a good thrashing."

"It will teach you," said Gram, "to show more respect for us."

Driblet nodded. "All right," he said. "Just be here tomorrow at sunrise."

THEY MET THE NEXT MORNING under a blue sky.

"Let's get started," Dram said gruffly. "It's going to rain before nightfall."

Driblet removed five casks from his cart. "Yesterday," he said, "you talked of emptying a barrel at one meal. A truly great drinker, I think, could empty these casks by noon."

Dram laughed. "Nothing to it," he said, opening the first. The rich smell of strong wine engulfed him. "This will be a real pleasure." He leaned back and poured the wine into his gaping mouth, tossing away the cask afterward. A second one soon followed it.

Dram wiped his mouth on his sleeve. "Delicious," he told them, staggering forward. He slowly lifted the third cask, twirled around twice, and sat down.

"Are we at sea?" he asked.

"Steady there," said Gram.

Dram quickly took another large swallow. "Good stuff," he insisted, licking his lips. "Very, very good stuff."

"And more yet to come," said Driblet.

"Plenty of time," Dram murmured, sprawling out across the ground, "after I get off the boat." He was snoring in seconds.

"Ah, well," sighed Gram, "he'll sleep till dark

for sure. So much for his boast. But that still leaves me. And a great eater doesn't drink while he eats."

"My thoughts exactly," said Driblet, lifting a crate from the cart and placing it in front of Gram. "It's not a suckling pig, but I tried my best. Undoubtedly, a great eater could empty this before the sun rises above the treetops."

Gram sniffed in disdain. "Of course," he replied.

"Go right ahead," said Driblet.

Gram pried off the crate's lid. "Crackers," he announced. "I like crackers." He crammed a handful in his mouth, crunching and munching with relish. "Nice and fresh," he mumbled.

He ate some more.

A short time later, he began edging toward the remaining casks of wine.

"Great eaters don't drink while they eat," Driblet reminded him.

"Bah!" spat Gram. "I know that." He crunched and munched even louder than before.

Driblet waited. Gram continued to stuff handful after handful in his mouth. The crate was not small, though, and the rising sun beat down upon him. Gram's mouth tightened. His cheeks sagged. He picked up a cracker and dropped it. He picked up another, studying it closely. The cracker was light, tasty, and yet . . . He abruptly crushed it between his fingers. The sun cleared the treetops as he stomped off into the forest.

Driblet allowed himself a smile and went inside to fix his roof.

Too Clever for Words

T HERE WAS ONCE a handsome town acclaimed for its excellence in every regard. Here were gathered skilled artisans, ingenious minstrels, gifted masons, and shrewd merchants, each plying their crafts from morning till night, and sharing jointly in the town's esteem. Everyone had a contribution to make; everyone, that is, except a single loafer named Gruffle. He could not sing or paint, write or draw; his sense of humor was coarse, and his manners were the same. The town boasted of many fine houses; Gruffle's was a shambles. Brass-buttoned waistcoats and velvet breeches were the fashions of the day; Gruffle preferred rags. His company, when it was tolerated at all, was endured because it was known that he had inherited a fortune from distant cousins. Gruffle, however, was not one to throw his money recklessly about.

Despite his unpopular status, Gruffle had never doubted his own worth. It troubled him, though, that his brilliance went unrecognized. When would the townspeople realize their mistake, he wondered?

He finally grew impatient with waiting. Grimly determined, he began poking into dark corners and eavesdropping on his neighbors. If he could find something amiss and then correct it, he thought he would earn widespread fame. On his fourth visit to the stodgy meetings of the Town Elders, a notion occurred to him. He sat up and chuckled delightedly.

"Do you wish leave to speak?" asked an imperious Elder, smiling privately to his colleagues. Gruffle's foibles were well known.

"I do, indeed," said Gruffle. He stood to address the chamber. "I have lately been examining the works and customs of our town. They are admirable in every respect but one. Our language. Words and phrases are only coarse tools in our mouths; we use wit as a seasoning instead of a main course. Why, any beggar speaks as well. But if we make an effort, this flaw can be purged from our midst. A little time and hard work could transform the speech of our people into the town's greatest accomplishment."

Rarely had Gruffle spoken at such length and, judging by the faces of his listeners, never had he made such sense. Applause swept through the room like a wave at high tide. In its wake, the Town Elders unanimously passed Gruffle's proposal and adjourned to put it into effect.

Amid countless smiles and congratulations, Gruffle departed in triumph. And the news spread quickly. He was widely hailed in the streets and pointed at from afar. "I must have finer clothes," he decided upon returning home. Rags hardly suited his new eminence. He removed a bag of gold from a dusty cupboard and went out into the town again.

The changes were already apparent.

"Extremely clement weather, eh, Master Gruffle?" said one passerby.

"A felicitous afternoon to you, sir," said another.

Gruffle reached the tailor's shop in fine spirits. "I have graced your establishment," he told the proprietor grandly, "in search of elegant daily attire."

"To be sure," said the confused tailor.

"Spare no expense," Gruffle added, revealing the bag of gold.

The tailor understood this plainly enough. He brought forth his finest silks and linens, spreading them out on a large table. With his guidance, Gruffle ordered three coats, four pairs of breeches, and a dozen shirts, all in the best materials to be had. He left the shop once the measurements were taken. The bag of gold remained behind.

From bedroom to ballroom and parlor to pantry, soon nobody went anywhere without a dictionary in hand. New witticisms were snatched up by the score, only to be discarded after a few days' use. Like a lighted candle, the brighter the remark, the faster it burned out.

Gruffle gleefully took more and more bags of gold from the dusty cupboard. His house was painted, servants were hired, the garden was weeded, and the furniture was dusted and polished. Testimonials were held in his honor and Gruffle began to entertain in turn, the better to give people the chance to praise him. And they did at first, for his parties were glittering successes, his food and drink as delicious as it was plentiful. But before long, he found the mood growing different.

"A splendiferous assemblage," he observed to a wealthy jeweler at one of his late night gatherings.

The jeweler took no notice, so intently was he memorizing a new proverb he had just heard.

Gruffle moved on to a circle of laughing merchants. "What induced this levity?" he asked.

"A superior jest," was the answer.

Gruffle asked them to repeat it, but they politely refused. Even a clever joke could not bear a second telling. The merchants laughed again and went off to refill their glasses.

A frown settled on Gruffle's brow. What had

become of his treasured compliments? Could it be that his famous proposal was eclipsing its creator? Such a thing must not be allowed to happen, he thought. If the originality of what a person said was now so important, then he must prove himself to be a peerless creator of unique phrases.

"Attention!" he shouted. "I admonish everyone to give heed to my next statement."

When the crowd had quieted, he announced a contest. To stimulate interest in the use of language, he was challenging one and all to debate him in the public square. It would provide a showcase for the cleverest speakers in town, he explained. After he wisely added that refreshments would be served, his guests cheered him delightedly.

ON THE DAY of the contest, a platform was constructed in the square, rimmed with banners that fluttered in the breeze. At either side stood ten long tables. Cooks and bakers soon appeared to cover them with trays of meats and pastries. Chairs were placed in front of the platform for the Town Elders, whom Gruffle had asked to judge the event.

The spectators were not long in arriving. The competitors—two professors, a peddler, three minstrels, and a little girl, who was there at her parents' prodding—gathered under a striped tent. Gruffle welcomed them heartily and led them to the platform.

Once the last scraps of food were gone, the contest began. The professors' mastery of words was impressive, but they were inclined to argue with each other rather than with Gruffle, and the Elders disqualified them. A discussion of trade and finance exhibited the peddler's experience, his glibness served him well there; but his vocabulary was not large in the area of art and literature, something Gruffle exploited to the full. The minstrels posed a greater threat. Gruffle was not their match in voice or lore; he knew enough, though, to invite them to sing their recent compositions. That was the deciding touch. The minstrels had not yet managed to weave tuneful melodies around intricate lyrics. Amid a flurry of jarring notes, the crowd heckled them out of contention.

This left the reluctant little girl.

Gruffle prompted her to speak. "Cast aside your apprehension," he said confidently. "Still your trembling appendages."

The girl shuffled toward him.

Gruffle smiled. "Shall we enumerate the virtues of herbivores?" he asked. "Or perhaps propose a parody of present perfidy?"

The Elders nodded approvingly.

The girl clutched her dictionary tightly, as though inspiration might pass through its covers

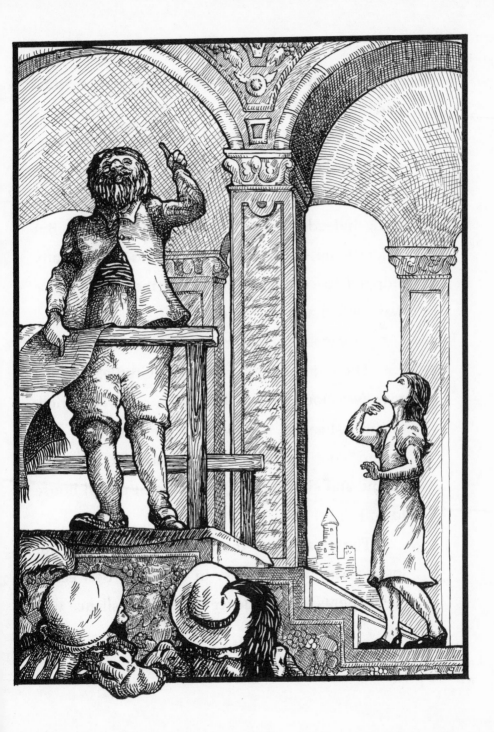

into her mind. But there was no inspiration to be had.

Gruffle talked blithely on while she stood petrified in his shadow. As dusk approached, the Elders conferred heatedly. Gruffle had spoken well; indeed, far better than anyone else. But whereas he paused for breath and occasionally stopped to collect his thoughts, the girl's silence was perfect and unbroken.

At sunset, the Elders declared her the winner.

Their announcement startled Gruffle. His outrage was boundless. "Despicable curs!" he cried. "Mutton-headed vagabonds! This travesty will hound you forevermore." He stalked home in shame and shut himself up in his beautiful house to sulk.

The meaning of the Elders' decision was not lost on the townspeople. In a contest between a clever phrase and a clever silence, the silence was clearly preferred. By nightfall, piles of dictionaries had been carted outside the town gates, never to return. After that, one could hear a pin drop in every home for years to come.

A Barrel of Fun

A WELL-DRESSED PEDDLER once stopped his wagon in a farmyard on the edge of the wild just as dusk was drawing on. The goods he carried filled the wagon, obviously wondrous things from many lands, and the man himself seemed to be a person who had traveled widely and seen much.

Outside the barn, a boy stood feeding the chickens, his hand scooping corn from a bucket with clockwork precision. Pout was his name, and he looked up warily at the peddler's approach. "What do you want, fellow?" he asked.

The peddler smiled benevolently and gripped his lapels. "Young man," he said smoothly, "you appear to be a bright lad. How far is it to the next inn?"

Pout put down the bucket, his expression suddenly alert. If this stranger had gold to spend at an inn, how much better it would be if he paid well to stay at the farm. Nothing would please his father more, he thought, than a chance to earn some gold. "None lies near," he politely replied, "but we have a guest room you are welcome to use."

The peddler quickly accepted the invitation.

Supper was served in the kitchen at a plain wooden table surrounded by stiff, straight-backed chairs. Pout's father, Nurlish, sat at one end, swallowing his food as fast as his knife could cut it. His wife, Glour, sat opposite him, picking at her plate like a forlorn bird. Neither of them spoke. It was not the boisterous setting the peddler might have

55

preferred, though it took nothing away from his appetite. He ate heartily, sharing a word or two with Pout whenever his mouth wasn't full.

"A fine place you have here," the peddler remarked, after the last piece of pie was gone.

Nurlish grunted.

"Have you had the farm long?"

"Long enough," said Nurlish. He yawned twice, got to his feet, and trudged off to bed.

"Pleasant dreams," the peddler murmured.

Glour soon followed her husband's example. Pout led the peddler to a small storage room where a rough cot had been hastily made up. The peddler pronounced it fit for a king, much to Pout's satisfaction, and they parted for the night.

AT BREAKFAST, Pout presented the peddler with a lengthy bill, carefully written out on foolscap. Pout was good at figures and looked quite pleased with his handiwork.

The peddler's face showed great concern. "Oh, dear," he muttered, stroking his chin. "This, too, is fit for a king."

"Any inn might charge as much," Pout insisted. "And you were looking for one only yesterday."

"I asked how far it was to the next inn. Nothing more."

"And nothing less, either," said Nurlish, as he and Glour cleared the table.

The peddler protested his innocence. He admitted to being short of funds, but insisted he was a fair man. "I suggest that we strike a bargain," he declared. "In my wagon is a large barrel, a barrel of fun. Take it with my compliments."

"F-U-N," said Nurlish.

"That's right."

Pout wanted to see it.

"Very well," snorted Nurlish. He picked up a halter strap and ran it through his fingers. "We'll judge for ourselves what kind of trade you're making."

Pout accompanied the peddler to the barn. Working together, they lifted down the barrel from the wagon, huffing and puffing all the while.

The peddler wiped his brow and patted the barrel affectionately. "A rare treat, this. Do you want a taste?" Without waiting for an answer, he pried off the lid and took out a ladle.

"Looks like water," Pout said suspiciously.

"Looks can be deceiving," the peddler replied. "Of course, it's all the same to me, but once your father takes a sip, he may not wish to share it."

Pout knew his father well enough not to argue. He dipped in the ladle and drank. An unfamiliar smile slowly spread over his face. "Sweeter than honey," he murmured.

The peddler cautioned him to be quiet.

"Shush! Shush!" said Pout. "Shush, cow.

Shush, chickens. Everybody shush!"

The peddler began hitching up his horse to the wagon. "I trust, Pout, that you're satisfied with the trade I've proposed."

Pout giggled.

"That's what I wanted to hear."

The peddler's hasty departure raised a cloud of dust that drew Nurlish to the barn in a hurry. "What happened, Pout?" he cried. "Why did you let him go? I would have taken the gold out of his hide." He clenched his fists. "With something to spare, I expect."

Pout shrugged, turned a cartwheel, and climbed into the loft.

Nurlish shook his head. "He made a fool of you twice, Pout. There's no excuse for that. Now, stop swinging from the rafters and come down here at once."

Pout did nothing of the sort. He swung back

and forth, giving no heed to his father's increasingly angry demands. Nurlish finally gave up, promised to deal with him later, and stormed out to the fields.

Pout dropped into the hay and went to sleep.

The midday meal was marked by his absence. This puzzled Glour, but when she asked Nurlish about it, he only grunted something about "fools doing as they pleased." That hardly satisfied her, so after he left, she wandered outside.

"Pout! Pout! Where are you?"

Nobody answered. She walked into the barn, where the unfamiliar barrel claimed her attention. One cautious sip from the ladle was followed by another.

"A bit of sparkle in that," sighed Glour. She thought at once of the daisy chains she had made as a girl, though why, she had no idea. The bright sunshine outside suddenly beckoned. Twirling around, Glour skipped out into the meadow, where the daisies were in full bloom.

A buzzing fly finally woke Pout. He yawned and stretched, pulling the hay from his hair. The chickens were squacking hungrily, so he climbed down from the loft and filled a bucket with corn. After drinking again from the barrel, he wandered into the yard.

"Here you go!" he shouted, throwing the corn high in the air. It rained down upon the surprised chickens, sending them scurrying for cover. They clucked at Pout from under the eaves. He ignored them.

"What are you doing?" asked his mother, returning from the meadow. Her cheeks were flushed and her hair tousled, the result of a fruitless chase after butterflies. A long daisy chain hung about her neck.

"Feeding the chickens, of course." Pout put

the now empty bucket over his head. "All gone,"
he murmured.

The chickens ventured out timidly and began
to eat.

"I wanted to ask you something," said Glour,
fingering the daisy chain. "But I don't remember
what." She licked her lips.

Pout grinned and followed her into the barn.

NO SMOKE CURLED invitingly from the chimney
when Nurlish returned home. He sniffed deeply.
No smell of cooking, either.

"What's going on?" he thundered, opening
the door of the house.

Glour turned away from the far window.
" 'Evening, dear," she said. "My, you look tired."

"I am. What's that around your neck? And
why . . . Who brought that barrel inside?"

"Pout and I did. Quite a job, too. But we

wanted to have it close by. Are you feeling ill, dear? You're very pale."

Nurlish scowled at her. "I'm hungry!" he roared.

"Don't shout, dear, you'll just upset yourself. Come watch the sunset with me." She turned back to the window and started humming.

At that moment, Pout came out of his room.

"Still grinning like an idiot," muttered Nurlish.

"Hullo, Father!" sang Pout. "Did you have a good day? No, don't tell me, I can see that you didn't." He dipped a mug in the barrel. "Have some of this, you'll feel better."

Nurlish grudgingly accepted the mug. He privately thought they had both gone mad, but he didn't want to alarm them. As he sipped, however, his frown began to unravel. "A daisy chain," he mumbled. "Haven't seen one of those in years."

He put his feet up on the table.

"Where's my pipe?" he asked shortly. "I haven't smoked it in ages."

Pout found a pipe and a pouch of tobacco in the cupboard. To his astonishment and delight, his father blew smoke rings up the chimney. And later that night, after a cheerful supper of toasted bread and cheese, Nurlish took Glour for a long walk under the stars.

They all overslept the next morning.

"Goodness!" exclaimed Glour, toppling out of bed. "It's almost noon."

"Nurlish yawned. "And what of that?" he said. "Let's take a holiday."

"We could have a picnic."

"We could, indeed," he replied. "Nothing like a little change now and then."

The barrel of fun was soon emptied, of course, but the memory of it lingered pleasantly, prompting other holidays from time to time. Not that the barrel itself was discarded. The curved wood was so well-suited to rocking that Nurlish made a cradle from it. When Pout grew older and married, his children were lulled to sleep in it, and their children after that. Never again was a barrel of fun seen in those parts, but every baby rocked in that cradle grew up with a fine sense of humor.

FIC
K KRENSKY, STEPHEN
   CASTLES IN THE AIR

DATE DUE

MAY 2 1			
107			
DEC 8			
108			
JOURY			
JAN 3			
205			
JAN 8			
207			